NEW TALES
OF
NASRUDIN

NEW TALES
OF
NASRUDIN

Eric K. Sorensen

iUniverse, Inc.
New York Lincoln Shanghai

New Tales of Nasrudin

iUniverse books may be ordered through booksellers or by contacting:

iUniverse
2021 Pine Lake Road, Suite 100
Lincoln, NE 68512
www.iuniverse.com
1-800-Authors (1-800-288-4677)

ISBN-13: 978-0-595-39802-7 (pbk)
ISBN-13: 978-0-595-84210-0 (ebk)
ISBN-10: 0-595-39802-2 (pbk)
ISBN-10: 0-595-84210-0 (ebk)

Printed in the United States of America

ACKNOWLEDGEMENTS

❀

The author is deeply indebted to the work of the late Dr. Idries Shah, the foremost 20th century authority on Sufism and compiler of hundreds of traditional tales of Nasrudin. The reader is strongly encouraged to read any work by Dr. Shah to learn more about Sufis.

INTRODUCTION

❦

Tales of Nasrudin have been used for centuries by the Sufis, a mystical form of Islam. The character of Nasrudin has been claimed by cultures from Turkey to Russia, and he can be seen to exemplify the most common foibles of humanity as well as the highest insights into the Divine. He is thought by many to be a fool, by others to be a saint; and as his tales delight and entertain the reader, opportunities for learning are available on multiple levels. It is said that a reading of seven Nasrudin stories consecutively will open the mind to a step on the path to Enlightenment.

These New Tales of Nasrudin are presented in that spirit and tradition.

TO EACH HIS OWN

Nasrudin was traveling with a caravanserai. He had just finished his evening meal and was suffering some indigestion when he was persuaded to take a walk with two others, a soldier and a pacifist dervish. As they walked Nasrudin's two companions argued their different points of view to the Mullah. Suddenly they came upon a tiger in the road that had been gorging itself on a freshly killed animal. The beast gave them a swift glance, then turned and disappeared.

"He left us alone because he could see that we meant him no harm", said the dervish.

"Nonsense!" countered the soldier. "I had my hand on my sword and gave him a look which scared him off!"

Nasrudin belched. "Perhaps he was as full as I am and didn't want to upset his stomach any further!"

IT'S MORE BLESSED...

Nasrudin was traveling through the wilderness with a companion. They had become lost and food was running low. Eventually they were down to the last morsel of food. They looked at the food, then at each other.

"It's more blessed to give than to receive", said the companion.

"In that case", said Nasrudin, "I will give you the blessing of giving me the food!"

MYSTICAL PHRASES

Nasrudin had a student who was expressing his frustration at what seemed to him the slow pace of his studies.

"Master, I have heard that there are certain key phrases which, once learned, open the gates of enlightenment and greatly accelerate one's ability to understand the divine mysteries."

"All right," said the Mullah. "We will begin tomorrow, and we will be joined by another student who is at a similar level of progress."

The next day the student arrived in a state of anticipation to find Nasrudin teaching the mystical phrases…to a parrot.

IT WOULD BE A LOT EASIER...

Nasrudin was shopping for a new donkey. He had heard of a dealer who had a beast for an unbelievably low price, and eager for a bargain he immediately visited the man and made the purchase.

He soon found, however, that this particular animal had an evil disposition. In his first attempt to take the donkey to the marketplace he was thrown, kicked, bitten, and had his foot stepped on. If he tried to lead the donkey one way it wanted to go the other, and it would not cooperate in having a load placed on its back. He happened to pass the stall of the donkey-seller in the midst of these travails.

"Ah, Mullah! Are you happy with your deal?" asked the rascal.

"The price was reasonable enough," answered Nasrudin. "As for the donkey: It would be much easier to handle if only it wasn't so difficult!"

SALESMANSHIP

Nasrudin decided he had to try to sell his donkey. But he was afraid no one would buy it because of its many negative qualities.

"Try a little salesmanship," suggested his wife. "Just emphasize the positive and try not to mention the negative. Then practice what you're going to say so it comes out just right."

Nasrudin left for the market, confident that with enough salesmanship he could easily sell this troublesome beast.

He returned very shortly, feeling pleased with himself…but still in possession of the selfsame donkey.

"Nasrudin!" cried his wife. "Weren't you able to sell it?"

"Oh, I could have sold it ten times over after I gave my sales pitch," said the Mullah. "In fact, I had a dozen men outbidding each other for the honor of owning this marvelous creature."

"Then why didn't you sell it?" sputtered his wife.

"When I saw how valuable this donkey was in the eyes of all those men, I decided it was too precious to part with!"

BLAME IS LARGELY CIRCUMSTANTIAL

On the front step of the Mullah's house sat an old doormat. It had served well for many years, but it developed a warp so that when Nasrudin was returning home from a walk he tripped over it and fell through his doorway.

As he got up and brushed himself off he admonished the doormat. "You may well be angry about your status in life, and I can applaud your desire to take a new form and function. I can even understand your desire for revenge against the thousands of times these shoes have rubbed their dirt off on you. But couldn't you have attacked them sometime when I wasn't wearing them?"

ROOTS CAN HAVE DISADVANTAGES

Nasrudin went to live for a while on the side of a mountain that was known to be an active volcano. One day the inevitable eruption occurred, and a lava flow proceeded down the slope directly toward the Mullah's hut. As he fled for his life he turned and called to the trees: "It's lucky for me that I didn't get as comfortable in this location as you, or I might have forgotten that I could escape the fate you are about to suffer!"

GIVER OF HAPPINESS

For a while Nasrudin took to calling himself "The Giver of Happiness". However, his behavior during this time was constantly irritating to everyone around him. He acted boorishly at the dinner table, dressed in rags and never bathed, refused to do even his basic chores at home, and insulted any unsuspecting person who dared try to have a conversation with him. Finally his wife asked him, "How can you call yourself 'The Giver of Happiness' when you seem to make everyone in your presence absolutely miserable?"

"Yes, but think how happy everyone is when they are not in my presence; which is a much greater portion of their lives than the moments they spend with me!"

HOW TO TEACH

Although Nasrudin had something of a reputation as a teacher, he was usually reluctant to take on a new student. If a new prospect told him, "I want you to teach me this:…" then Nasrudin would likely tell him that his schedule was too full for another pupil. Likewise for any candidate who would say, "I want to know all that you know."

Every once in a while someone would approach Nasrudin and say, "I don't really understand anything about anything. I thought I did, but I guess I really don't know what I'm doing."

Nasrudin would answer, "Well, I don't really know what I'm doing either, but maybe if we do it together we can both learn something!"

TRYING TO BE AUTHENTIC

Nasrudin occasionally applied for jobs that seemed interesting to him, but he was turned down at the conclusion of the interview every time. A friend advised him, "Nasrudin, you are not dressed properly. One look at you and the interview might as well be over!"

"But I have no other clothes. What should I do?" the Mullah wailed.

"I will borrow a proper suit from a friend of mine. I'm sure he'll let you use it for the interview. Then, when you get the job you can give it back to him and buy your own suit with your first paycheck."

Nasrudin wore the borrowed suit to the next interview that came up, and as it happened, he got the job and started immediately.

His behavior at work, however, was distressing to his co-workers. He made his eyes bulge out of his face, waved his arms about wildly, spoke in a loud, harsh voice, and reeled about the workplace until he bumped a table and knocked it over.

"Nasrudin!" his employer cried. "What is the matter? Why are you acting like that?!"

"I confess!" shouted the Mullah. "These are not my clothes, and I do not know the owner, so I didn't know how to behave in them, and I got confused!"

IT MUST BE PHEROMONES

Nasrudin had a nephew who had studied insects at the university. The young man was trying to explain how scientists had discovered that insects of the opposite sex were automatically attracted to each other by means of chemicals called pheromones. He pointed out that a male moth could be drawn to a female from over two miles away.

"The poor devils!" exclaimed the Mullah. "And I suppose that they have no idea what hit them until the effects wear off and they are being processed by the divorce courts!"

FATHER AND SON

When Nasrudin was a child, he did not get along well with his father. The young Nasrudin kept a personal account of his father's sins and foibles, and resolved to himself that he would not repeat those mistakes and thus would lead an improved life. Among those traits of his father that most annoyed Nasrudin was his habit of loudly snoring at night, keeping the rest of the household awake. After many a sleepless night Nasrudin would glare resentfully at his father in the morning. "How unjust that he enjoys the comfort of a full night's rest at our expense!" he would mutter to himself.

As Nasrudin grew older he remained estranged from his father, until it had become taken for granted that the father and son simply did not get on well with each other.

One night Nasrudin awoke to find his wife shaking him and saying, "Nasrudin! Your snoring is keeping the whole neighborhood awake! Can't you please turn over and sleep in a different position?"

The Mullah leapt out of bed and started to dress.

"Whatever are you doing?" exclaimed his wife.

"There's not a moment to lose! I must go see my father at once! I have wasted many years of perfectly good anger on a man who did not deserve it, and I must ask his forgiveness."

"What, at this hour?"

"Well, if I can sleep through my own snoring, I must find out if I can also sleep through his. And perhaps he may not be able to sleep through mine!"

BASEBALL

A traveling exhibition baseball team stopped at Nasrudin's village, and a crowd soon gathered to watch this curious activity. In a short time a reasonable facsimile of a baseball field was set up in a broad flat area, and soon the villagers were treated to a demonstration of the sport. Not that they understood any of it: the players would run on and off the field, they would throw and catch the ball, and sometimes a player with a heavy club would hit the ball. They carried on until they reached some predetermined point, then they declared the game over.

Many of Nasrudin's neighbors were a bit disconcerted by it all. What did it mean? Was it some form of blasphemy?

The Mullah was unperturbed.

"This is obviously a group of traveling dervishes, and they are practicing a form of sublime, if somewhat arcane, dancing movements. Let us treat them with respect and offer them food, for they are on a holy path."

ONE HUNDRED MILES PER HOUR

The pitcher of this group of baseball players wanted everyone to know that he was capable of throwing the ball one hundred miles per hour.

"Indeed?" said Nasrudin. "Baghdad is exactly 100 miles from this spot! If you can throw your ball from here to there in one hour, that would be something I would like to see very much! The only problem is, I would have to be able to run 100 miles in an hour in order to watch!"

THREE STRIKES

This same pitcher challenged anyone who dared to try to hit the ball when he "pitched" it. And there was no doubting that he could throw the ball with amazing velocity. The "batter" would get three "strikes", or chances to swing the bat at the ball.

Much to the amusement of the assembled audience, Nasrudin volunteered. He stepped forward and grabbed a bat. As he approached the plate, however, he seemed to lose confidence, so that by the time he stood in the batter's box his knees were shaking and he could barely hold up the bat. When the pitch came blazing in he cringed and took a halfhearted swing that missed the ball entirely. The crowd laughed. "Be careful, Nasrudin! Don't hurt yourself!" they shouted. The Mullah held up his hand for silence. "I was merely demonstrating a man who was thinking too much about what others had told him, and thus was so afraid to fail that he had no chance to succeed."

The crowd watched closely as Nasrudin approached the plate again. This time he glared menacingly at the pitcher and pounded his bat on the plate. By every appearance he was ready to pulverize the ball. He gave a mighty swing at the pitch, but the result was only a weak pop-up.

Nasrudin turned to the crowd. "That was a man who thought he could overcome a challenge with aggressive behavior. He was too out of balance to accomplish anything."

He then stepped back into the batter's box and matter-of-factly hit the next pitch over the outfield fence and out of sight.

"And who was that?" asked someone as Nasrudin strolled off the field.

"That?" The Mullah smiled. "That was me!"

KEEN EYESIGHT

Nasrudin had a niece who was head over heels in love with a young man who had rather an unsavory reputation. In spite of that, she extolled his virtues to her uncle, listing what she thought to be his many good qualities. After listening for awhile, Nasrudin took her by the hand out to the camel barn, gave her a pitchfork, and asked her to start digging through the manure. "But, Uncle," asked the puzzled girl, "what is it I am seeking?"

"I'm not sure myself," said the Mullah, "but with your highly developed powers of perception I'm sure you'll discover something of value!"

SUFFERING

When Nasrudin would hear of someone else's misfortune he would sigh and shake his head. "We are all meant to suffer in this world," he would say. The time came when he had a streak of bad luck himself, and much to everyone's annoyance, he complained bitterly to anyone who would listen. Finally someone took him to task.

"Nasrudin, I though you said we were meant to suffer."

"That's true," said the Mullah. "But how will anyone know I'm suffering if I don't complain about it?"

IF YOU WANT FLIES

Nasrudin had been in a bad mood. His wife said, "You know, you'll get more flies with honey than with vinegar."

"If it's flies you want," said the Mullah, "nothing works like a big pile of manure!"

ATTITUDE

Nasrudin had a friend who had been born into a wealthy family. This fellow seemed to get one good break after another, and some people felt he had enjoyed more than his share of good fortune. However, he got involved in a business venture that went sour, and he suddenly found himself in trouble with the authorities. He came to Nasrudin for advice.

"Yes, I can see that you have problems," said the Mullah. "But did it ever occur to you that you have led an unusually lucky life? If you were so willing to accept the good, shouldn't you now be prepared to deal with the bad?"

"So in other words," said the friend, "I deserve what's coming to me, and I should just go bankrupt and end up in prison?"

"Tsk-tsk. Now, now," said Nasrudin. "Don't be so negative!"

INCONSIDERATENESS

Nasrudin himself ran afoul of a certain king and was thrown into prison. He was able to convince his jailers to release him for a day in order that he not miss an important appointment. When Nasrudin arrived at the appointed time and place, however, the person he was to meet was nowhere to be found. The Mullah waited, and waited, and waited, until very nearly at the end of the day the other party finally showed up.

"I apologize for my tardiness," he said. "I was unavoidably detained."

"Don't try to appease me with your excuses!" thundered Nasrudin. "Had I known you would be this late I could have stayed in jail most of the day!"

JOB SECURITY

The king who had imprisoned Nasrudin was overthrown and replaced by his more liberal-minded nephew. The new ruler immediately released Nasrudin and placed him in charge of the cellblock containing the roughest, most hardened criminals.

"Surely a man of his enlightenment will impart a sense of compassion and spirituality to these men, especially after his own experience as a prisoner," thought the monarch.

However, he began to get reports that the Mullah was mistreating his charges almost to the point of cruelty: denying them visitors, giving them poor food, and haranguing them at every opportunity. The king had Nasrudin brought before him to account for his behavior.

"Why do you mistreat these men so? I would think you would at least show them some gratitude, for were they not in prison you would not have a job."

"Yes, that is so," answered the Mullah. "But they did not get into prison because people were nice to them, did they? I'm only trying to make sure I'll always have a job!"

DETERRENCE

The new king had an advisor who wanted to implement a plan to improve the health of the populace. He felt there were far too many people engaged in unproductive, harmful habits involving intoxicating substances. He petitioned the king for laws to stamp out this sort of activity by having anyone caught with illegal intoxicants being thrown into prison, with all their possessions being forfeited to the government.

The Mullah Nasrudin happened to be present in court as the king was hearing this proposal. He noticed a fly that had landed on the advisor's turban as he was making his presentation. Nasrudin leapt forward and delivered a tremendous blow to the speaker's head, sending him sprawling to the floor. However, he missed the fly, which disappeared out a window.

"What is the meaning of this?" cried the king.

"Your Majesty, flies are carriers of pestilence and pose a great danger to the well-being of the kingdom," explained Nasrudin. "If the learned counselor was injured by my excessive use of force, that is a small price to pay for the message that the fly will take back to his fellows. We won't be bothered by them anymore!"

IF YOU LOSE YOUR WAY…

Nasrudin was riding his donkey through a mountain pass in a blinding snow-storm. He was having trouble finding his way when he noticed some tracks in the snow ahead of him. He urged his mount to follow them with haste, which the beast did…right over a small embankment and nearly on top of the trav-eler who had made the tracks.

"Fool!" shouted the stranger. "It's bad enough that I lost my way and fell off the path! Now you almost kill me!"

Nasrudin sniffed indignantly. "Well, if you're going to get lost, the least you could do is not leave any tracks for others to follow!"

WHAT IF...

Nasrudin was walking along the road one day when he spotted something shiny in the ditch. Closer examination revealed it to be a beautiful piece of jewelry.

"This must be worth a fortune!" he thought. "At last, all my troubles are over!" He picked up the treasure and hid it under his cloak.

As he continued his journey, Nasrudin began to think about what he would do with his newfound riches. He realized that it would be difficult to explain how he came by this thing of value, and the possibility existed that he would be accused of stealing it. The great value of the gems began to weigh on him, and the thought of theft made him realize that there could be robbers on the road who would think nothing of slaying him for the jewels.

With every step he became more nervous and unhappy, until finally he could stand it no longer. He took out the object and threw it out of sight.

"Whew! That was close!" he exclaimed. "If I had held onto that for any longer, there's no telling what might have happened!"

PROCRASTINATION

Nasrudin had a habit of putting things off until the last minute, then becoming frantic as the deadline approached. A friend observed to him that the stress involved in this lifestyle could affect Nasrudin's health in a bad way.

"Your procrastination will be your undoing if you don't change your ways," he warned.

As it happened, there was something Nasrudin had to get done the following week, and the friend decided to pay the Mullah a visit to see if his advice had had any effect. He found Nasrudin sitting calmly, serenely sipping tea.

"So, it appears you have heeded my advice and completed your task on time," said the friend.

"Not at all," answered the Mullah. "It was the worrying which was making me unhappy, and the worrying was a direct result of my procrastination. So I've decided to put off my procrastinating until next week!"

LOST AND FOUND

One of Nasrudin's neighbors was walking past the Mullah's house when he saw something in the yard outside the window. Closer inspection revealed it to be a family heirloom which, although it had no intrinsic value, was known to be of great sentimental importance to Nasrudin. The neighbor picked up the item and knocked on Nasrudin's door.

The neighbor was rewarded by the look of joy on the Mullah's face when he saw what was being returned.

"Ah!" exclaimed Nasrudin. "I'm so glad to see that! I thought I might never see it again!"

The neighbor continued on his way with a sense of satisfaction. On his way home he again passed Nasrudin's house. He was surprised to see the same object lying in almost the same place outside the window. He returned it to the Mullah and received the same enthusiastic response.

"But, Mullah," He asked, "I just returned this to you a few hours ago. How is it that you lost it again so quickly?"

Nasrudin gave him a wink and walked over to the window, opened it and tossed the object into the yard.

"There is great joy in possessing something of value," he explained, "but the joy is multiplied when that item is lost and then found again. I have no way of knowing that any passerby will return it, so my happiness is enhanced by each instance of human trustworthiness."

Just then there was a knock at the door.

"Mullah, I found this in your yard and knew it means a lot to you..."

"Ah, thank you, thank you, thank you!" said Nasrudin.

LIBERTY

Nasrudin found himself at one point to be in the employ of a king as an advisor. The monarch went to great lengths to make the Mullah feel that he was needed: He gave him his own office with a full staff, a salary the likes of which Nasrudin had never seen, and free access to the royal presence at any time.

"Of course," said the king, "If this is not to your liking you are free to go whenever you wish."

Nasrudin immediately donned his cloak and made for the exit. The king was stunned.

"Haven't I given you everything you could possibly hope for?" he exclaimed.

"If you feel you have the authority to grant me my freedom you may at some point decide you have the authority to take it away," said Nasrudin. "I think I'll leave before you change your mind!"

DO AS I SAY

Nasrudin was going to take his children to a field to pick berries. His wife gave him specific instructions before they left:

"Make sure you tell them not to eat all the berries while they pick them, or we won't have any to save."

"Yes, dear," said the Mullah dutifully.

When they returned, there were hardly any berries in the baskets, the children's faces and clothes were stained with berry juice, and their little stomachs were so full that they hurt. Nasrudin's wife was incensed.

"Husband, didn't you say you would tell them not to eat the berries?"

"I did!" protested Nasrudin. "But I don't think they could understand me with my mouth full!"

MAKING A POINT

Nasrudin overheard a former soldier announcing that he was turning away from his military training and seeking a path of non-violence.

"I renounce violence and conflict in all its forms," stated the man. "I elect to live a life of peace from this moment forward!"

Without warning Nasrudin let out a bloodcurdling scream and hurled himself at the soldier as if to do him great bodily harm. The startled man instinctively put a fighting hold on the Mullah, then threw him through the air to land with a thud in the roadside, where he lay senseless for a few moments.

As he was being helped to his feet, someone asked: "Mullah, whatever were you doing to attack that man?"

Nasrudin shook his still groggy head and winced at pains in places he didn't know he had. "I think I was trying to make a point, but I'm not sure why I wanted to be right!"

OWNERSHIP

When Nasrudin was a young man, he moved to a new village where his reputation as a holy teacher had preceded him. It was not long before he was visited by some of the elders. They gave him an appraising look-over, talked with him a while, then declared him fit to be their chief cleric.

Nasrudin politely but firmly refused.

"But, why?" they asked. "We had heard of your keen insights and your ability to interpret the scriptures according to Allah's will. Are we unworthy of your attention?"

"Not at all," said Nasrudin. "You have a certain image of who I am which causes you to make this request. However, I have not yet attained ownership of this image, and therefore it is I who feel unworthy of the task you wish for me. I could offer to buy this idea of who I am from you, but then you would no longer have it, and so you would not want me anymore."

A young boy had been peering in the door and observing all. To everyone's surprise he piped up. "What if we could share it with you?"

Nasrudin accepted the job, on the condition that the boy be made his assistant.

INSPIRATION

Nasrudin went to a teahouse with some friends one evening. There was a singer performing: a man of moderate talent and less than mediocre ability, who had a personality and presence that was most unendearing. When he had completed a particularly horrific rendition Nasrudin approached him.

"I wish to thank you for your singing! It is quite inspirational! In fact, I would say you are directly responsible for some of the best music I have ever heard!"

As the Mullah's party prepared to leave, they asked him: "Why in the world did you complement that man so? His singing was pure torture to sit through!"

Nasrudin smiled. "I happen to know that one of the most successful musicians in the land once came here before he began his career. He had always loved music but was unsure whether he wanted to pursue it as an avocation. When he saw this fellow get up and do what he does, he thought, 'If this guy can be a performer, anyone can, including me!' Had he not had this man to inspire him, the world would have missed the joy of his fully developed talent."

HUMILITY

For a time Nasrudin behaved in a very egotistical manner, much to everyone's annoyance. He went on at great length about his many accomplishments, his virtues, and in general, what a fine specimen of humanity he was and how fortunate the world was that he was a part of it.

Finally someone suggested that he try to exercise a little humility.

"Yes, I had just thought of that," answered Nasrudin. "Fortunately there is no one better at humility than I am!"

WHAT HAPPENED TO THE VIEW?

One day during his travels Nasrudin came upon a place in the wilderness of unsurpassed beauty. Before him lay a clear lake in which was reflected a snow-capped mountain, blue sky and fleecy clouds. The shore was lined with towering trees, hundreds of years old.

"I must stay awhile and absorb this fantastic scene," declared the Mullah, and he constructed a humble lean-to from which he had a clear view of the lake.

While Nasrudin sat in contemplation of the greatness of Allah's creation, a band of travelers arrived on the same spot. They, too, were struck by the immense beauty and decided to stay. They set about cutting down a few trees with which to build some cabins.

Word of the scenic lakeshore spread to the over-crowded city, and before long the place was teeming with tradesmen, farmers, animals, a market, and construction was begun on a new mosque.

The lake was dotted with boats, and it was becoming befouled with waste from the new village. The forest was rapidly disappearing, and smoke from a hundred fires filled the air and obscured the mountain from view.

Nasrudin packed up his things and made for the road.

"Mullah! Where are you going?" cried the people.

"I had a beautiful view, but I seem to have misplaced it," answered Nasrudin. "If I find it again I think I will leave it alone so that it might not be lost again."

PERFECTION

For awhile Nasrudin worried about each little mistake he had made in his life. Sometimes he would fret out loud over some minor character flaw he had noticed in himself. His wife tried to console him.

"Don't worry so much. After all, nobody's perfect!"

Nasrudin smiled and shook his head. "Ah, but I'm so close!"

IN THAT CASE...

Nasrudin had loaned a family member a sum of money. A long time passed, and no mention was ever made of the debt. Nasrudin began to grow concerned that the money would never be repaid, and he prepared to take the matter up in the courts to get his money back. Then he realized that this was probably too harsh, and that if this relative was not able to repay the sum, then Nasrudin should not make life any more difficult for him. He paid his relation a visit to let him know the loan was forgiven.

"But, Nasrudin," said the fellow, "I was just getting ready to pay you back!"

"Well, that's different!" said the Mullah, and demanded his money back immediately.

IS THIS THE WAY?

Nasrudin was sitting in front of his house, talking with a friend. A traveler stopped and asked if he was on the right road to Baghdad.

"Yes, of course you are," answered the Mullah. "Just keep going."

A little while later another stranger stopped and asked if he was on the right way to Mecca. "Indeed, yes," said Nasrudin. "Just follow the road."

Not long after a dervish stopped to ask if this was the route to Damascus. Nasrudin assured him that it was.

His friend seemed puzzled. "How can this road be the way to all those places at the same time?" he asked.

"Well," said Nasrudin, "That's the road I have to take whenever I want to go someplace. In fact, it's the only road to anywhere from here!"

CORRECT THYSELF...

Nasrudin was watching a friend working at a task. He noticed a way that the job might be accomplished more easily, so he spoke up. The friend saw that Nasrudin was right, changed his method, and indeed the job went much more easily. The friend thanked Nasrudin profusely.

Encouraged by this instance, Nasrudin began pointing out flaws, incorrect ways of doing things, and what he perceived as injustices to everyone he met. It got to the point where nobody wanted to see him coming or speak to him at all. Finally, one of his few remaining friends decided to discuss this issue with the Mullah.

"I am so grateful to you for telling me this!" exclaimed Nasrudin. "I had realized that my greatest flaw was my habit of correcting others, but I didn't know how to tell myself about it without telling myself about it!"

IMAGINATION

One morning Nasrudin's neighbors awoke to find him perched on the edge of his roof. Although it looked as though he would topple to the ground at any moment, the Mullah seemed not the least bit concerned. In fact, he gazed about himself with an air of complete ennui.

"He's lost his mind!" cried one person.

"No, he's practicing some strange art he learned in a heathen land," said another.

"Maybe he is demonstrating his disdain for the corporeal plane and his devotion to the spiritual," said a third.

Finally they approached and asked Nasrudin what he was doing.

"I am trying to determine," he said slowly, "whether imagination was developed as a response to distress or boredom."

BUBBLES

Once Nasrudin passed some time with a group of children who were playing with bubbles. They could make clouds of little bubbles, filling the air with shimmering, sparkling globes. They also had a large wire loop that could make huge bubbles.

One particularly large bubble caught an updraft and floated toward the sky. However, before it could get completely clear it hit the branch of a tree and popped.

Nasrudin shook his head and smiled. "It's a tough world for bubbles," he said.

PEOPLE, THINGS & IDEAS

A visiting cleric was preaching to Nasrudin about the evils of gossip.

"Great people speak about ideas," he said, "Mediocre people speak about things, and little people talk about other people."

Nasrudin considered this. "What of those who have ideas about other people's things?"

PARANOIA

For a time Nasrudin made his home in a small mountain village. When he first moved there, it seemed the natives were suspicious of strangers. He had numerous encounters in which he had to speak quickly and calmly in order not to be violently attacked for what seemed to be no reason at all. He became increasingly nervous and suspicious himself until one day he was set upon by three villagers and thoroughly beaten.

As he lay moaning on the ground, the Mullah started to laugh. "For a while there I thought I was paranoid, but now I realize everyone really was out to get me!"

CRITICISM

One day a friend of the Mullah's rounded a corner to find Nasrudin in conversation with another person. Suddenly Nasrudin became very excited, then angry, shouting and waving his arms. Then he turned on his heel and stormed away, fuming and muttering.

Nasrudin's friend caught up with him. "Mullah, whatever is the matter?" he asked.

"The nerve of that guy!" sputtered Nasrudin. "He said I don't take criticism very well!"

I SAY, YOU SAY

At times Nasrudin would look at his wife and say, "Oh, my dear, you know I feel that I don't treat you as well as I should."

She usually would respond, "Please don't worry about it. I know you are trying your best."

But once she said, "No, you don't treat me well enough…not nearly well enough!"

Nasrudin bristled with anger. His wife noticed and said, "Well, why do you get angry when I merely agree with what you just said?"

"When I say it, I'm being humble," said the Mullah. "But when you say it, it becomes an accusation!"

OTHER PEOPLE'S IDEAS

A friend said to Nasrudin, "I just heard a study that said that people have a natural resistance to the ideas of others, even though those ideas might be correct."

"That's ridiculous!" exclaimed the Mullah.

"WHAT I DON'T LIKE ABOUT YOU IS…"

Someone once said to Nasrudin: "What I don't like about you is that you behave so strangely!"

The Mullah said, "How interesting! That's about the only thing I like about you!"

PSYCHIC POWERS

Nasrudin met a dervish on the road. "Where are you bound?" asked the Mullah.

"I am on my way to a gathering of masters of psychic powers!" proclaimed the dervish.

"You mean to say you can actually communicate by means of telepathy?"

"Certainly!" asserted the dervish.

"Then why bother with the complication of traveling?" said Nasrudin, and continued on his way.

HALF EMPTY OR HALF FULL?

Nasrudin and a philosopher were in the middle of a debate. The philosopher, in order to make a point, picked up his drinking glass and challenged the Mullah: "Now, tell me, is the glass half empty or half full?"

"It looks dirty to me," said Nasrudin, "and I see that a fly has landed in it. To tell you the truth, I'm really not thirsty!"

PATIENCE

Nasrudin's wife left him with the children for the day. "Are you sure you'll be all right?" she asked.

"Of course!" he answered. "I have plenty of patience."

When she returned she found the poor Mullah disheveled, exhausted, and hoarse from yelling at the children. "I thought you said you had lots of patience!" she scolded.

"Yes, I do," muttered Nasrudin. "I just didn't say how long it lasted!"

BIGOTRY

"There's one kind of person I simply cannot tolerate," proclaimed Nasrudin, "and that's a bigot!"

THINK FOR YOURSELF

A young man applied to Nasrudin to become a student. He explained that he had studied under many other teachers and had been a diligent pupil of each of them. As proof he recited from memory the main points of his previous masters' teachings.

Nasrudin said, "I have but one rule for you to live by, and if you wish to be my student you must attend to it rigorously."

"Yes, Mullah, anything," exclaimed the young man.

"You must not listen to me, but you must think for yourself," said Nasrudin.

"But if I obey you, then I won't be thinking for myself...but in order not to obey you I would have to do the opposite, which would be to listen and obey, which would then make me..."

"Figure it out for yourself!" said the Mullah. "When you have, then perhaps we can discuss further studies."

GENDER BIAS

The Mullah's wife once complained, "I feel you don't respect what I say because I'm a woman."

"Oh, no, my dear, that's not so at all!" protested Nasrudin.

"See, you're doing it again!" cried the wife. "Isn't that just like a man!"

FIRST IMPRESSIONS

A long-time friend of Nasrudin's noticed that whenever the Mullah met someone for the first time he would behave with almost perfect decorum…"almost" because Nasrudin would invariably do something like pick his nose, scratch his crotch, or loudly break wind.

"What is the meaning behind this behavior?" the friend asked.

"I simply got tired of having to live up to first impressions!" answered Nasrudin.

SMALL AUDIENCE

For a time Nasrudin gave regularly scheduled lectures. They were never really well attended, and one evening the Mullah entered to find a single person in the audience.

"Mullah, please don't trouble yourself. I can come back when there are more people."

"It is you who should not trouble yourself. What you hear me say would be the same were there a hundred people here. And besides," smiled Nasrudin, "I have lectured to smaller groups!"

TIMING IS EVERYTHING

Nasrudin once was introduced to a man who had written his autobiography at the age of 80. The author had led a full and interesting life and had attained some prominence in the world, so the book had become a bestseller.

"Just think!" said the Mullah, "If only you'd written your autobiography when you were twenty you'd have had sixty years to collect the royalties!"

"MIGHT AS WELL BE ALIVE…"

Nasrudin happened to get caught in a winter storm without adequate clothing. He felt his body getting colder, starting at the extremities.

"I must be dead," he thought, "since bodies don't cool off until after the person has died!"

Like any respectable dead person would, the Mullah laid himself down on the ground. He immediately noticed that the cold ground was extremely uncomfortable. As he lay there the snowflakes tickled his nose, a rock dug into his back, and he worried that no one would find him to give him a decent burial before his corpse was devoured by wild animals.

"That does it!" he exclaimed. "What's the point of being dead if one still has to suffer and worry? I might as well be alive!"

"YOU MIGHT INQUIRE…"

Nasrudin once had a discussion with a Buddhist.

"If one is shot with an arrow, it matters not who fired the shot, but only that the wound be healed," said the monk.

"You might at least ask the shooter if he has any more arrows!" countered the Mullah.

NATURAL TENDENCIES

Nasrudin was visited by a friend who complained about nearly every aspect of his life: His wife didn't understand him, his children were rebellious, his boss was domineering, and the bankers and lawyers were out to bankrupt him. Besides that, the summers were too hot and the winters too cold, his house was falling apart, and his body was beginning to suffer the infirmities of old age. Nasrudin listened in silence. Then he went and got his pet cat, placed it at his friend's feet, gave the friend a stick, and suggested the friend try to play "fetch" with the creature.

"But, Mullah!" protested the friend, "Cats don't play fetch!"

"Is that so?" answered Nasrudin.

Moral: If you want to play fetch, play with a dog.

ALL OF THEM

Someone once asked the Mullah Nasrudin, "Which was the best sermon you ever gave?"

The Mullah seemed puzzled. "Which one? Why, they were *all* the best!"

ONE-WAY TRIP

A friend observed Nasrudin struggling to fit a large piece of firewood into his wood heater. As the Mullah wrangled and maneuvered the chunk into the chamber, the friend said:

"It would seem that that piece of wood is too big. Do you think it will burn all right?"

"Yes, it's a large piece, I'll grant you that. But I've noticed that in all the years I've thrown chunks of wood in this furnace, not one has ever come back out!"

RELIGION AND HAIR

Nasrudin once met a Sikh, who noticed the Mullah's long hair sticking out from under his turban.

"Why do you let your hair grow so long?"

"For religious reasons," answered Nasrudin.

"Ah, it is the same with me!" said the Sikh, his eyes alight as he fingered his braids.

"So, you don't wish to be mistaken for a Buddhist, either?" asked the Mullah.

RAMIFICATIONS

"Mullah, I just heard on the news today that scientists have developed a mouse that can live for forty years!"

"And what will the poor cats eat in the meantime? Nobody thinks of them!"

PAST/PRESENT

Nasrudin once received as his guest a prominent cleric who was known for his conservative outlook.

"All that we need to know has already been given to us!" declared the visitor. "The modern viewpoint can add nothing to the old teachings!"

When they sat down to the meal, Nasrudin served what could only be described as a mass of putrefying garbage. The old cleric was dumbstruck at first, then when he regained his speech he completely forgot his manners.

"Is this how you show hospitality to a guest?" he quavered.

"I don't understand!" exclaimed Nasrudin. "This meal was perfectly nutritious when I prepared it last week!"

A MATTER OF PERSPECTIVE

Nasrudin and a scientist friend were standing outside on a clear night, looking up at the sky. As they gazed at the glory of the Creation, Nasrudin's friend began to expound.

"We stand on a planet which is nothing more than one of billions and billions of grains of sand on the Beach of Eternity. The light from those stars has traveled across unfathomable distances over hundreds and thousands of years to reach us! It really makes you think about your place in the Universe, doesn't it?"

"Indeed it does!" said the Mullah. "Imagine! Traveling all that way just to reach *my* eyes!"

SUCCESS

A friend once asked the Mullah Nasrudin if he felt he had achieved any measure of success in his life.

"Success? Why, I have been successful at nearly everything I have attempted. When I was president of my own company…"

"Do you mean to say that you were a businessman?" the friend asked incredulously.

"Yes. In fact, for a while I was making quite a lot of money, which was quickly spent on status symbols. And although I was capable of the hard work required to maintain my position, the stress began to affect my health. In addition, there was a spiritual price to be paid in order to run the business successfully. Eventually I chose to follow a different path."

The friend still seemed doubtful. "If you are so good at everything, why are you just getting by?"

"Yes, I am just getting by," said Nasrudin. "But you have to admit, I'm pretty good at it!"

WHAT A SILLY QUESTION!

"Mullah, do you talk to yourself when you're alone?"

"Well, in order to talk to myself, I would have to be with myself, and if I was with myself I wouldn't be alone, would I? So the answer is no: what you ask is manifestly impossible!"

SUICIDE

"Mullah, have you ever thought of suicide?"
"Why go to the bother of killing yourself when the world is perfectly willing to do it for you?"

MISTAKES

"It is said we learn from our mistakes."
"That would qualify me as a genius!" said Nasrudin.

DOING HIS PART

Nasrudin was asked: "What are your thoughts on the Women's Movement?"
"I fully support equality in all aspects of the economy, politics, society and the family." he answered firmly.
"I would further state that I like women in general, I enjoy their company in particular, and I wholeheartedly support the concept of peaceful coexistence between the sexes as a fundamental need for the survival of the human race." The Mullah sighed. "And it would seem that my present role in that endeavor is to live alone!"

SEX

"Mullah, I beg your forgiveness for my impertinence, but what are your views concerning sex?"

"If you are referring to sexual intercourse as an act of pleasure between two consenting adults, I feel it is an activity that achieves greatest success when performed by people who know each other very, very well...or by total strangers!"

AS OLD AS THAT?

Nasrudin found a gray hair in his beard. "Oh, I'm getting old," he moaned.
"Mullah, you're not so old!" said a visiting friend, who coincidentally happened to be about the same age.
"I'm older than I've ever been in my entire life!" countered Nasrudin.

THE DIFFERENCE IS OBVIOUS

Through some clerical error Nasrudin was for a time employed by the tax department. He was told to examine a proposal to tax tobacco products and offer suggestions, especially as they pertained to the deleterious effects to the health of tobacco consumers.

After reading the proposal the Mullah commented, "I agree that we must heavily tax tobacco snuff, because the snuff itself causes direct damage by its contact with the mouth and throat. However, I do not understand why we tax cigarettes, cigars, and pipe tobacco at all. After all, is it not the smoke that is harmful? The tobacco itself causes no harm until it is lit. Therefore we must also heavily tax matches and lighter fluid, and we shall need to find a way to tax the smoke!"

VERY GENEROUS

Nasrudin was walking and talking with a friend. He spoke mostly of his problems, frustrations, aches and pains.

The friend, known to be somewhat pious, remarked, "Well, you know of course that suffering is a necessary part of spiritual growth."

Whereupon Nasrudin turned and gave his companion a swift, forceful kick in the rear end.

The astonished man could barely sputter, "What in the world was that for?"

"Your sagacious words gave me such insight and revelation that in my enlightened state I had no choice but to share with you the gift of spiritual growth!"

QUESTIONS & ANSWERS

Nasrudin worked for a time at a school as a teacher. His students regularly scored higher on their tests under his tutelage, which caused a stir among the rest of the staff, who generally considered him to be a simple fool.

One day the Principal was observing in the classroom and noticed that the Mullah would sometimes give a clearly incorrect answer to what seemed an easy enough question. He took Nasrudin aside and asked if he was aware of what he was doing.

"Certainly," he answered.

"And exactly why do you deliberately mislead the students of this school?"

"Well, for one thing, they learn not to believe everything they hear, and they learn how to look things up and check each answer twice!"

TRUTH

Nasrudin once said: "I have found that those most in need of the truth are also the least receptive to it. Therefore I make sure to include a number of half-truths and outright lies in my teachings. Those who would believe anything will continue in their blissful state of self-delusion…it's the best I can do for them. There are some, however, who can see more clearly and may eventually find their way to the Truth."

AN HONEST MAN

"A truly honest man," said the Mullah, "is one who will tell you about every time he has lied."

WHY DON'T PEOPLE LIKE ME?

Mullah Nasrudin had been in a depressed mood for a while. He felt he could do nothing right and that his life was doomed to failure.

"Why don't people like me?" he wailed to one of his few remaining friends.

"Well, you know, it's difficult for people to like you if you don't like yourself," suggested the friend.

"How could I possibly do that?" moaned Nasrudin. "I could never like someone who doesn't like himself!"

THE PUBLIC POOL

The first time Nasrudin saw a public swimming pool he stared fascinated for hours.

The friend who had brought him took him to task. "Mullah!" he chided, "Surely you aren't taking some sort of impure pleasure from the state of undress of the swimmers?"

"Not at all," said Nasrudin. "I was just noticing how most people stay in the shallow end, where they splash and play games. The few who inhabit the deep end of the pool have highly developed skills in swimming and diving, and they tend to be comfortable on their own."

"I see," said the friend. "And where, may I ask, would we find you in the pool?"

"Why, swimming laps, of course!"

A MATTER OF PRINCIPLE

Nasrudin was speaking with his nephew about the young man's prospects for gainful employment.

"I don't know what I want to do," said the nephew, "but it doesn't really matter, since money is not important to me."

"A very noble principle," said the Mullah, "and one which you will find most employers are more than happy to help you carry out in practice."

EQUANIMITY

Nasrudin had a friend who prided himself on his liberal values and his sense of toleration.

"I treat everyone exactly the same, regardless of their background, race, religion, or social standing." he declared.

"Really?" said the Mullah. "It's been my experience that the only persons who can truly do that are those who hate everyone!"

SPEAKING IN GENERALITIES

"The only certainty in life is that nothing is certain.

"The one thing all people have in common is that each of them is a unique individual.

"I find it best *never* to speak in generalities!"

HUMANISM

Nasrudin had a friend who was a mental health counselor and who ascribed to the humanistic point of view.

"I believe all human beings have an inherent capacity to choose what is best for themselves," he declared.

"But if that were true," said the Mullah, "wouldn't you be out of a job?"

UPSIDE DOWN

A friend passing Nasrudin's house found him outside standing on his head.

"Hello, Mullah. What are you doing?"

"I'm trying to hold up the world," said Nasrudin, his face red and his eyes bulging.

"Hold up the world?"

"Yes! I have heard it said that the world is a huge ball that is forever falling through empty space, and I'm just trying to do my part to hold it up!"

"Mullah, with all due respect, that's ridiculous!"

"Well, you might think so," said Nasrudin, "but that's only because you're upside down!"

EXERCISE

"Mullah, what do you do for exercise?"
"I wrestle demons."

PROBABILITIES

Nasrudin went to see a doctor about a pain in his side. The doctor took some blood and ran some tests.

"It will be a few days before we get the results back," he said, "but I would say there's only a twenty per cent chance that it's something serious."

"From where I see it," said Nasrudin, "it's either 100% that it is serious or that it's not!"

DENIAL

Nasrudin was talking with a friend who worked in a clinic dealing with the issues of mental health.

"One of the biggest problems," said the friend, "is the attitude of denial."

"If you're implying that I'm in denial over some issue or another," said Nasrudin indignantly, "let me assure you that I'm not!"

IT TAKES ONE TO CATCH ONE

Nasrudin found himself traveling through a land where it was the custom to avoid eye contact at all times, especially with members of the opposite sex. He walked along with his eyes cast downward, never daring to look anywhere near the face of anyone he encountered, for he had heard that transgressions of this custom were severely punished.

However, along the way he saw a woman of great beauty approach, and in spite of himself he felt his gaze drawn to her face for a brief glimpse. He found her staring directly back at him.

"Ah-ha!" she exclaimed. "I caught you looking at me! We'll have the authorities deal with the likes of you!"

"Is that so?" said the Mullah. "It would seem that I caught you as well. I'm a stranger in this land and unaccustomed to the discipline necessary to conform to your ways, but what's your excuse?"

IGNORANCE

"The problem with ignorance," said Nasrudin, "is that those who are afflicted have no idea of the extent to which they are afflicted."

HERE WE ARE!

Nasrudin was approached by a student who declared: "I wish to follow you so that I may attain the goal of enlightenment. Will you assist me on this path?" Nasrudin answered, "Here we are!"

The student was puzzled by this, but resolved to discover the meaning and told the Mullah he would return the next day to begin his studies.

When the student arrived at Nasrudin's house the Mullah again exclaimed, "Here we are!" and immediately set out on the road. The student hurried after him. Nasrudin went to the market and bought a few vegetables and sweets. The student watched closely, but he could see nothing more in the transaction than what appeared on the surface. The pair left the market and left the village, making for a nearby mountain.

He means to take me to a sacred spot on the mount, thought the student.

Halfway there, the Mullah stopped to rest and eat the food he had bought. "Here we are!" is all he would say.

After several hours journey they reached the bottom of the mountain. "Here we are!" said Nasrudin. Then instead of climbing he walked around to the other side. Once there he again declared, "Here we are!"

"Master, are we not going to ascend to the summit?" asked the confused disciple.

Without a word the Mullah started upward, not stopping until they had reached the peak. Nasrudin gazed at the splendid view stretching out before them. "Here we are!" is all he would say. Then without further ado he descended. He continued straight on until he reached his home. As he entered, he turned to the exhausted and perplexed student and said, for the last time, "Here we are!" and closed the door.

NASRUDIN THE BAKER

Nasrudin worked for a time as a baker. He became famous for his delicious pastries, cakes, breads, muffins, and piecrusts; in short, anything he baked seemed to turn out perfectly.

"What's your secret?" he was asked.

"It's really quite simple," answered Nasrudin. "I merely ask the dough what it wants to be, then I use my skills to make it the best it can be."

THE MYTH OF THE CAVE REVISITED

Nasrudin was engaged in a discussion with a philosopher.

"It is the duty of all enlightened persons," said the savant, "to lead their fellow men out of the dark cave of ignorance."

"True enough," said the Mullah. "But you may want to bear in mind that they have become accustomed to the darkness, and you will need their guidance when you enter the cave from the light outside. Likewise, be aware that the brilliance of enlightenment will be painful for them to perceive until *they* are able to adjust."

VISIONARIES

"The key to productive creativity," said Nasrudin, "is the ability to distinguish between a vision and a hallucination."

BARGAINS

A friend noticed that Nasrudin had been leaving his home early each morning for the past two weeks, not to return until late at night. He asked the Mullah the purpose of these journeys.

"I'd heard that a market in a village a half-day's trip from here sold figs at a lower price than we pay locally."

"How much cheaper?" asked the friend.

"Two pennies a pound."

"And how much do you buy?"

"Enough for my meals as I travel, and with the money I save I'm able to buy feed for my donkey!"

MINDS AND TEACUPS

A Zen master once said to Nasrudin, "A mind is like a teacup: No learning can take place if it is already full."

"How true," said Nasrudin. "And what if it is cracked?"

POWER

The Sultan had heard a rumor that he was considered no more than a figurehead and that the true power in his kingdom resided elsewhere. He summoned Nasrudin to court in order to use his perceptive abilities to ascertain the truth of this matter.

"Mullah, who is the most powerful person in the land? Is he in this room?" asked the Sultan.

"He is not," said Nasrudin.

The Sultan was shaken. "Do you know who he is, and can you take me to him?"

"Follow me," said Nasrudin, as he made for the dungeons. He stopped outside a cell deep in the bowels of the prison.

"This is ridiculous!" cried the Sultan. "This prisoner is not a rebel leader or even a prominent criminal. He is a common thief, and is condemned to die on the morrow! He has no power whatsoever!"

"Does he not?" said the Mullah. "If such as he did not exist, you would have no one over whom to exercise the power of life and death. It is true that he will die tomorrow, but another will take his place, and another, and another. The strong cannot exist without the weak to dominate, so I ask you, what is the true source of power?"

NOT AS BAD AS I THOUGHT

A friend passing Nasrudin's house saw him out in the front yard, wandering as if he did not know where he was. Further inspection revealed that the Mullah had wrapped his turban so low on his head that his eyes were covered. The friend approached.

"Hoy, Nasrudin! Are you all right?"

"Who is that?" cried Nasrudin.

"It is I, your neighbor."

"And where am I?"

"You are in your front yard, Mullah."

"Oh, thank Heavens! I'm not nearly as lost as I thought I was!"

PSYCHOANALYSIS

A well-known psychoanalyst stopped by Nasrudin's house on his way to a conference. He intended to study the Mullah's reputed peculiar behavior and try to arrive at a diagnosis. After a few hours of questioning he prepared to leave.

"Can you tell me how to get to Baghdad from here?" he asked.

"Well," said Nasrudin, "where did you start from?"

The man answered.

"And what route did you take along the way?"

Again the man answered.

"Why did you choose that particular route?"

"I don't understand the question," said the psychoanalyst.

"Ah, perhaps that has something to do with how you feel about your mother," said Nasrudin.

"Sir," said the indignant man, "I only wish to know how to get to my destination from here!"

An equally indignant Mullah responded, "And I only wish to inform you in a manner which is familiar to you!"

ONLY HUMAN

Once again, Nasrudin was in a funk, feeling down about himself. His wife tried to cheer him up.

"You're too hard on yourself," she said. "After all, you're only human!"

"I know," said the Mullah, "It's just that sometimes I wish I weren't *so* human!"

GREAT READING

A well-known academic researcher gave Nasrudin a copy of his publication, a book that he had spent ten years researching. A month afterwards, he asked the Mullah if he had got anything out of the book.

"I find it to be one of the most useful books I have ever owned! It has truly improved the quality of my life!" exclaimed Nasrudin.

"Really?" said the author, quite flattered. "Well, you know, I was quite meticulous in the detail of my research."

"That could very well be," said Nasrudin. "All I know is that whenever I have trouble sleeping, I start reading your book and I am sound asleep in a matter of minutes!"

FISHING

Nasrudin was fishing with a friend. He had been sitting for a long time without any success, using a small worm and a bobber. He reeled in his line, removed the hook and float, and replaced them with a lure the size of a small mammal.

"Mullah!" his friend said. "I don't think there's any fish in these waters big enough to take that bait."

"Well, if I'm not going to catch anything anyway, I might as well not catch something worth bragging about!"

SHORT ANSWERS

"Mullah," asked a student, "life is so complex and ambiguous. Is it really possible to obtain the larger knowledge by learning small lessons?"

"Yes and no, and yes," said Nasrudin.

ASTROLOGY

Nasrudin once visited an astrologer.

"Tell me the date, time, and location of your birth, and I will reveal to you aspects of your personality and ways in which the planets and stars influence your life," said the seer.

"I have a better idea," said Nasrudin. "Follow me for as long as you deem necessary and observe me closely; then, based on your observations, tell me the date, time, and location of my birth. *Then* we'll talk!"

PURELY BY INTENTION

Nasrudin was out walking with a friend. The Mullah was wearing a light shirt, and the weather suddenly turned very cool. His friend was concerned.

"Mullah, I have an extra sweater if you like. I'd hate for you to get accidental hypothermia at your age."

"Hmmph! 'At *my age*,' if I get hypothermia it will be intentional, not accidental!"

MAKING IT ALL UP

A philosopher was conversing with Nasrudin on the topic of the nature of reality.

"Our notion of truth is merely a construction of the human mind. One man's good is another man's evil, within each perceived problem is the potential for a perceived solution. We're really just making it up as we go."

"Quite right," said Nasrudin. "However, let us not ignore the Truth which is a product of God's imagination."

SAND CASTLES

Nasrudin found himself at the beach. He spent his time constructing elaborate sandcastles, with the most intricate attention to detail. All sorts of people stopped to admire his work.

One of them asked, "Why do you put so much effort into these projects? Surely you realize that the tide and the wind will destroy them in a few days at most?"

"But you have now seen them, and the tide and wind will take much longer to undo your being, will they not?" said the Mullah.

EVERYBODY'S A CRITIC

Nasrudin got it into his head that he wanted to learn to play the clarinet. He obtained an instrument and began a diligent regimen of practice. From the sound of the first note his dog began to whine and howl loudly. Finally, Nasrudin stopped playing and said, "I know exactly how you feel! I'd be complaining myself if I didn't have this clarinet in my mouth!"

INSOMNIA

One night at bedtime, Nasrudin's wife requested that he help her wake up before sunrise so she could get an early start on a trip to her mother's house in a distant village. He nodded absently, and then became engrossed in his thoughts and musings as he lay in bed. Time passed, and Nasrudin could not quiet his mind enough to sleep. To add to his troubles, he began to worry about staying up so late he would oversleep and not get his wife up on time, and he would have to suffer her wrath. Of course, these thoughts only contributed to his insomnia.

Finally he told himself, *There are only 3 hours to sleep before you have to get up. Go to sleep now!!* And, to his own amazement he did just that and woke up at the appointed time to avoid oversleeping. He was explaining this to his wife as she prepared to leave, and she exclaimed, "So you had to wait until then to realize you were only going to get three hours of sleep?"

"Exactly!" said Nasrudin. "Any earlier and it wouldn't have been three, would it?"

CENTRALLY LOCATED

Nasrudin had recently moved to a new home, and he extolled the location to some friends. "It's only a 10 minute walk to the market, and ten minutes to the mosque, and ten minutes to the tea-house. And, it's only a ten-minute walk to the park by the river! I would have to say that this house is perfectly centrally located!"

"But didn't you say the same thing about your other home, except because of its location it was a *fifteen* minute walk everywhere?" one of his companions smirked.

"Ah, yes. Well, you know, I've noticed that the center of the Universe seems to follow me everywhere I go!" said Nasrudin.

DO YOUR BEST

"All any one can really do," Nasrudin said to a student, "is your best."
"But what if one's best just isn't very good?" asked the student, who had been struggling with his understanding of the Mysteries.
"Try," said the Mullah, "not to do too much."

STAGE FRIGHT

Nasrudin was preparing a student for a musical performance. The young lady confessed that she was feeling very nervous, and indeed seemed about to lose physical and emotional control.

"What's the worst that could happen?" asked the Mullah.

"People will think poorly of me."

"Are you saying that you are capable of controlling the thoughts of others?"

"Well, no…but I could be causing their bad thoughts!"

"Here are some techniques that may help," said Nasrudin, and he suggested she visualize her performance beforehand as if it were really happening and experience the fear so she could become accustomed to the extra adrenaline.

"Why do you play your instrument?" he asked.

"Because I enjoy it," she replied.

"And why did you choose to perform in public?"

"Well, I really like this piece. It touches my soul."

"Then focus on *that*," said Nasrudin. "Think about the joy you have with this music and the chance you have to share it with others."

"Oh, Mullah!" she exclaimed. "That helps *so* much! I'd never looked at it that way before."

"And," said Nasrudin, "I'll be there in the front row to see how well my advice has helped!"

NASRUDIN THE PAINTER

A visitor to Nasrudin's house found the Mullah painting the ceiling, humming and dancing as he rolled the paint across the surface.

"Hello, Nasrudin! I thought you always said you hated painting the ceiling!"

"Yes, but that was before I discovered the opportunities for spiritual and practical wisdom that can be gained from this activity!"

"Really?" said the friend, somewhat skeptically.

"Certainly," answered Nasrudin. "Overcoming one's reluctance to perform a distasteful task is always good discipline; physical labor to improve one's surroundings is a way to serve Allah; and the appreciation of an attractive job well done contributes to mental and spiritual well-being!"

"I see," said the friend. "And the practical wisdom?"

Nasrudin pointed to his bespattered face and beard. "Never paint the ceiling with your mouth open!"

978-0-595-39802-7
0-595-39802-2

Printed in the United States
60723LVS00004B/18